may each page remind you of
how beautiful you are.

Look for beauty
with your heart!

You're beautiful when
you're thoughtful,

acting with thought shows others you care.

You're beautiful when
you're sweet,

your sweetness brings smiles.

You're beautiful when
you're playing...

Having fun just being a kid!

You're beautiful when
you're adventurous,

exploring the terrain and getting dirty.

You're beautiful when
you're laughing,

*letting your joy and delight overflow
from your smile.*

You're beautiful when
you're loving,

your inner light shines so bright...

So very bright.

You're beautiful when
you're singing,

*because some songs
shouldn't be sung alone.*

You're beautiful when
you're dancing,

*expressing your happiness and
the joy of life.*

You're beautiful when
you're creative,

bringing your imagination into reality.

You're beautiful when
you're trying,

your efforts count more than you know.

You're beautiful when
you're teaching...

There is so much we can learn from you!

You're beautiful when
you're brave,

*showing the world your strong and
courageous spirit.*

Shhhhhhh...

You're beautiful when
you're sleeping,

resting yourself for another day to come.

You're beautiful when
you're dreaming,

*creating positive visions in your
wild and wonderful mind.*

You're beautiful when
you're believing.

Hold on tight, it strengthens your path.

You're beautiful when
you're you,

*that's when you're
the most beautiful of all...*

You, beautiful you.

About the Authors

Stefanie Fields is a Certified Hypnotherapist and spokesperson for self-esteem and empowerment. She firmly believes in setting a vision, trusting your path, and working hard toward your goals.

Be bold in your actions and sincere in your ways. Use what you've been given! Do what you're meant to do. Life will surprise you and, best of all, you just might surprise yourself.

Phyllis Howard is an award winning artist working with graphite, color pencil, and acrylics. She enjoys pencils as easy tools that provide exquisite challenge and enjoys acrylic due to its versatility in application. Her passion is in the process of creating.

Your dreams want to come true; that's why they chose you.

Made in the USA
San Bernardino, CA
09 August 2017